Asterix the Gladiator

Gaul was divided into three parts.
No, four parts – for one small village of
indomitable Gauls still held out against the
Roman invaders . . .

Asterix the Gaul and his mighty friend Obelix
become gladiators in ancient Rome and invent
a few new rules for the Grand Circus Games.
'Above all the adventures of Asterix are
enormous fun.'

(Margery Fisher, *Growing Point*)

D0784312

TEXT BY GOSCINNY

Asterix the Gladiator

DRAWINGS BY UDERZO

Translated by Anthea Bell and

Derek Hockridge

 KNIGHT

The paperback division of Brockhampton Press

ISBN 0 340 16806 4

This edition first published 1973 by Knight, the paperback
division of Brockhampton Press, Leicester.
Second impression 1974
First published in Great Britain in 1969 by Brockhampton Press Ltd

Text copyright © 1964 Dargaud S.A.
English-language text copyright © 1969 Brockhampton Press Ltd

Printed and bound in Great Britain
by Richard Clay (The Chaucer Press) Ltd
Bungay, Suffolk

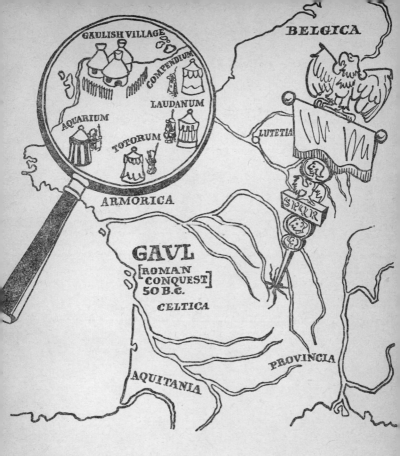

The year is 50 BC. Gaul is entirely occupied
by the Romans. Well, not entirely. . .
One small village of indomitable Gauls still
holds out against the invaders. And life is not easy for the
Roman legionaries who garrison the fortified camps of
Totorum, Aquarium, Laudanum and Compendium . . .

Now turn the book sideways
and read on . . .

a few of the Gauls

Asterix, the hero of these adventures. A shrewd, cunning little warrior; all perilous missions are immediately entrusted to him. Asterix gets his superhuman strength from the magic potion brewed by the druid Getafix...

Obelix, Asterix's inseparable friend. A menhir delivery-man by trade; addicted to wild boar. Obelix is always ready to drop everything and go off on a new adventure with Asterix – so long as there's wild boar to eat, and plenty of fighting.

Getafix, the venerable village druid. Gathers mistletoe and brews magic potions. His speciality is the potion which gives the drinker superhuman strength. But Getafix also has other recipes up his sleeve...

Cacofonix, the bard. Opinion is divided as to his musical gifts. Cacofonix thinks he's a genius. Everyone else thinks he's unspeakable. But so long as he doesn't speak, let alone sing, everybody likes him...

Finally, Vitalstatistix, the chief of the tribe. Majestic, brave and hot-tempered, the old warrior is respected by his men and feared by his enemies. Vitalstatistix himself has only one fear; he is afraid the sky may fall on his head tomorrow. But as he always says, 'Tomorrow never comes.'

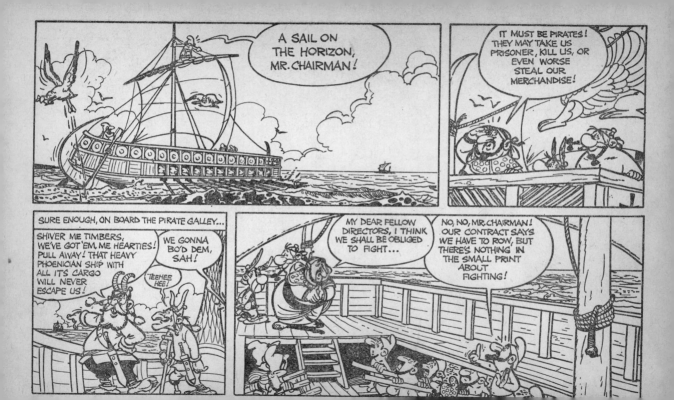

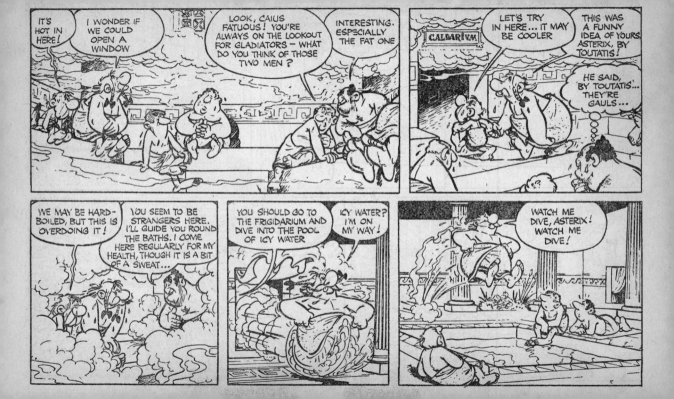

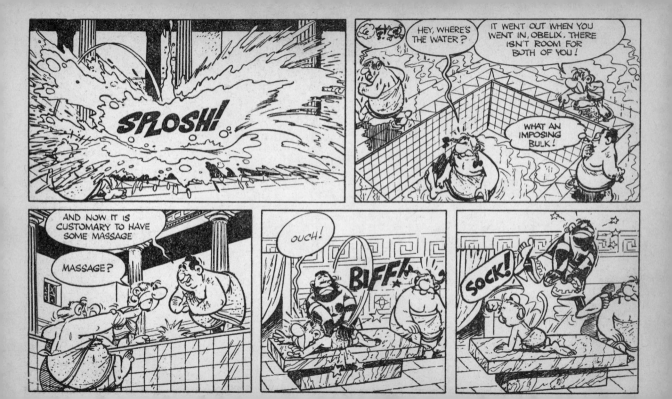

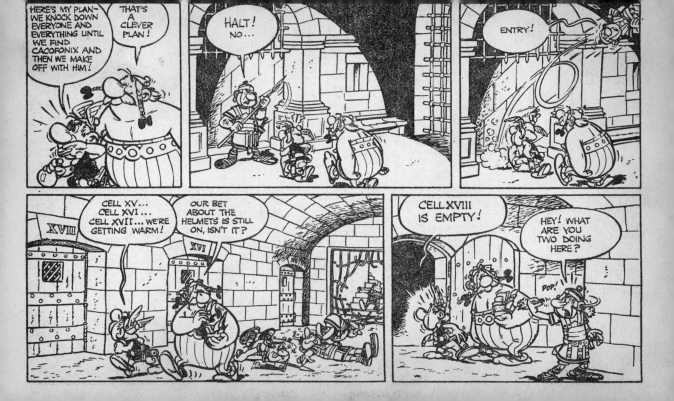

TEN THOUSAND SESTERTII
FOR THE CAPTURE OF TWO DANGEROUS INDOMITABLE GAULS: ONE SMALL FAIR MAN, BIG MOUSTACHE, WINGED HELMET, ONE FAT GINGER-HAIRED MAN, BIG MOUSTACHE, PIGTAILS
CAIUS FATUOUS
LANISTA.
IN THE CIRCUS INN...
OBELIX, I'VE JUST HAD AN IDEA! WE'LL BECOME GLADIATORS!
OH?
AND HOW DO WE GET TO BE GLADIATORS?
WE'LL ASK A ROMAN... THE ONLY ONE WE KNOW IS THAT ONE WHO HAS A LOT OF BATHS. LET'S GO TO THE BATHS!
AND OUTSIDE THE BATHS...
THERMAE
10,000 SESTERTII... THAT'S A LOT OF MONEY!
TEN THOUSAND SESTERTII
I COULD JUST DO WITH THAT!
LOOK!

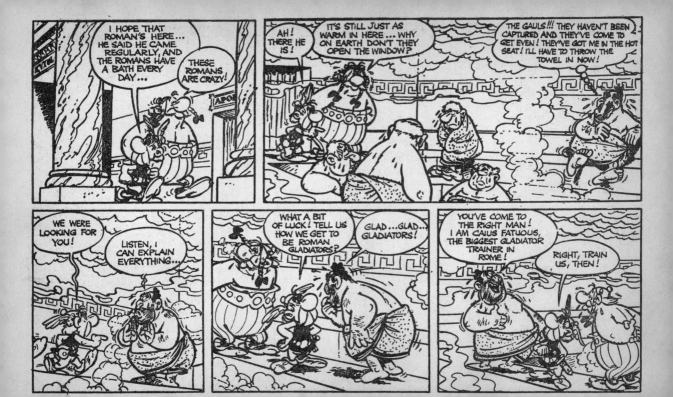

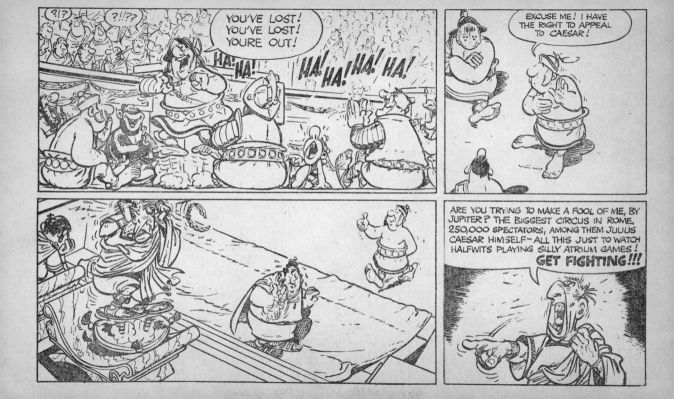

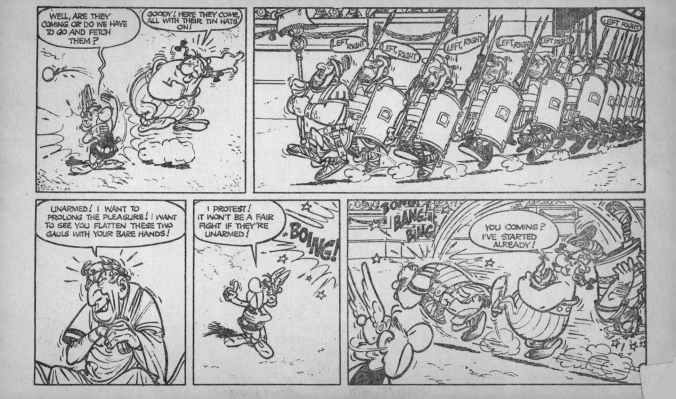